# HEIDI

# INTRODUCTION
## by Hayley Mills

The first time I read *Heidi* I must have been 10 years old.
I have never forgotten it, so I was delighted to have this
excuse to read it again, and again; I could not put it down.
It is a beautiful story and surprisingly powerful. It blos-
soms in your imagination and fills your heart and, in the
best, most subtle way, influences the way you feel about
life because it is about love, the power of love, the posi-
tive active influence of love in our lives.

It is a simple story – Heidi as a small child has nobody left
in the world who wants her. She is taken to live with her
rather frightening old Grandfather who lives a solitary
life high up in the mountains of Switzerland. Little by
little, by the sheer force of her personality, Heidi trans-
forms his life and the lives of all the people she encounters; but she is not remotely yukky, she is spunky and
terrifically courageous.

You meet marvellous characters that become completely
real. Taken away from her beloved mountains to the
dark, drab city of Frankfurt, shut away from the sunshine
and the sound of the wind and the fir trees, Heidi be-
comes a companion of Klara, a girl confined to her
wheelchair. Their friendship and the ultimate change in
Klara's life, the household and all the people that Heidi
encounters makes one see how much we all influence
other peoples' lives without ever realizing it and how
wonderful it is when it is for their good.

It makes me so happy that this very special story has been given a whole new lease on life by this beautifully produced and illustrated edition.

# HEIDI

**Illustrated by**
**DONNA PACINELLI**
**Story by JOHANNA SPYRI**

The Unicorn Publishing House
New Jersey

Edited by Heidi K. L. Corso, Kathleen Pizar, and Jacque Isherwood-Martin
Printed in Singapore by Singapore National Printers Ltd.
through Palace Press, San Francisco, CA.
Reproduction Photography by the Color Wheel,
New York, NY

♦ ♦ ♦ ♦ ♦


For information, contact Jean L. Scrocco at
The Unicorn Publishing House, Inc., 120 American Rd.
Morris Plains, NJ 07950.

♦ ♦ ♦ ♦ ♦

Distributed in Canada by Doubleday Canada, Toronto, ON

♦ ♦ ♦ ♦ ♦

Printing History 15 14 13 12 11 10 9 8 7 6 5 4 3 2

♦ ♦ ♦ ♦ ♦

Library of Congress Cataloging-in-Publication Data
Spyri, Johanna, 1827-1901.
(Heidi, English)
Heidi / illustrated by Donna Pacinelli
p. cm.
Translation of :Heidi
Summary: A Swiss orphan is heartbroken when she
must leave her beloved grandfather and their happy
home in the mountains to go to school and to care for an
invalid girl in the city
ISBN 0-88101-079-0:
(1. Grandfathers – Fiction. 2. Mountain life – Fiction.
3. Orphans _ Fiction. 4. Switzerland – Fiction.)
I. Pacinelli, Donna, itt. II Title.
PZ7.S772Ham 1988
(Fic) – dc19
87-30194 CIP AC

## CAST OF CHARACTERS

Heather Corrigan • Heidi
William Smergut • Grandfather
Devin Corrigan • Peter
Christina Sporer • Klara
Susan M. Gabrielson • Dete
Dennis Corrigan • Herr Sesemann
Margaret Lee • Grandmother
Margorie Murphy • Fraulein Rottenmeier, Grandmamma
James Marshall • Doctor
Sandy Gabrielson • Teacher
Barbara Desmond • Student
The Homeyer Goats • Goats

# LIST OF ILLUSTRATIONS

# HEIDI

From the pretty old town of Dorfli, a path goes up through green meadows. Soon it comes to the foot of mountains that look down upon the valley. Anyone who walks the path will soon smell fields, for the path goes up straight and steep to the Alps.

One sunny June day, a tall, strong-looking woman led a little girl by the hand up the path. In spite of the hot sun, the child was dressed in clothes for cold weather. She could not have been five years old, but no one could tell how big she was. She wore two or three dresses, one over the other, and a hot red scarf around her neck. Her feet were lost in heavy boots. From the long, hot climb, her cheeks glowed rosy-red under her dark brown skin.

After an hour of steady climbing, the two came to the town of Dorfli. A large kind-looking woman called from a doorway, "Wait a moment, Dete, I'll go up with you." The lady stopped and the little girl took away her hand and sat down.

"Are you tired, Heidi?" asked Dete. "We are almost there."

"No, I'm hot," said the girl.

As the kind-looking woman joined them, Heidi jumped to her feet. She followed the two women who had begun to talk.

"Dete," said the newcomer, Barbel, "where are you taking the child? It is your sister's little girl, isn't it — the orphan?"

"Yes it is," said Dete. "I have just had a very good job offered to me in Frankfurt and the child can't go with me. I am taking her up to her grandfather. She will have to stay there."

"What! The little girl is to live with the Alm-Uncle? You must be crazy, Dete! The old man will not want her to live with him."

"I have had her until now," said Dete, "and I can't think of letting her stop me from taking such a good job."

"I'm glad I'm not in the child's place," said Barbel. "The Alm-Uncle will have nothing to do with anyone! He never goes to church and never speaks to anyone. Once a year, he comes down with his thick walking stick and everyone keeps out of his way."

"Nevertheless," said Dete, "he is her grandfather and he must look after the child. He will not hurt her."

Dete recalled that it was after Heidi's father died that the Uncle went up to the Alm and stayed there, angry with God and man.

As the women talked, Heidi walked over to see a boy

Heidi's Uncertain Future

named Peter and his goats. The boy jumped about in his light pants and bare feet. At once, Heidi took off her extra dresses and put them into a neat heap. She danced with joy in her light little slip as she followed Peter.

Barbel had to see Peter's mother about some spinning, so she said good-bye. After Barbel left, Dete looked for Heidi. When she saw the girl, the aunt screamed, "Where are your things?"

Heidi pointed to a pile of clothes below.

"Peter, run back for me and get Heidi's things," said Dete. He brought the clothes. They all made their way with the goats up the Alm.

The Uncle sat by the side of his hut. Heidi went straight to the old man. She held out her hand and said, "How do you do, Grandfather?"

"Good morning, Uncle. I bring you Heidi, your granddaughter. She must stay with you," Dete said sharply. "You haven't seen her since she was a year old, while I have done my duty by her these past four years. Now it is your turn."

"Suppose the child begins to fret or whine for you, Dete."

"That is your problem."

At this, the Uncle rose angrily. "Go then, and don't show yourself here again for a long time."

"Good-bye, then; and good-bye to you, Heidi," said Dete. She hurried down the mountain as fast as she could.

After Dete left, the Uncle sat down. He blew great clouds of smoke from his pipe. Heidi looked around.

An Unexpected Obligation

She stood under the fir trees behind the hut. She listened to the wind sing through the branches. Then she came back and stood in front of her grandfather and said, "I want to see inside the hut."

"Come along, then," said the grandfather, "and bring your clothes."

"I don't want them anymore," said Heidi. "I'd rather go about like the goats with their fast little legs."

"She is not stupid," he said, half to himself. "So you shall," he said aloud, "but first bring your things inside and put them in the cupboard."

Inside was a good-sized room with a table, chair and bed. In one corner was a fireplace with a kettle. Everything the uncle needed was in the one cupboard: clothes, dishes and food. Heidi pushed in her clothes bundle as far back as she could.

Heidi looked into every nook and corner of the hut. She noticed a little ladder which led to the hayloft and quickly climbed it. There lay a fresh, sweet-smelling heap of hay. Through a round window one could look to the valley far below.

"Oh, Grandfather!" cried Heidi, "I shall sleep here!"

"Very well," said her grandfather. Gathering more hay, he made a thick bed and tucked a sheet over it.

"We have forgotten the blanket," said Heidi.

When grandfather found a cloth sack to put on top, Heidi declared, "The whole bed is lovely!"

Next they had a simple meal: a bowl of goat's

A Brand New World Begins

milk, thick bread and golden cheese toasted in the fireplace on the end of a long fork. Heidi sat on a three legged stool. She held her bowl of milk and drank and drank, for all the thirst of the long trip came back to her.

After they had eaten, the grandfather made a high stool so the little girl could sit at the table. Then he went about the hut with hammer and nails. He mended away wherever it was needed. Heidi followed him, for everything he did was fun for her to watch.

As evening came, the wind began to blow harder and harder among the fir trees. They moaned through their thick tops. Heidi was very happy and skipped and jumped under the firs as if she was having the best time of her life. The grandfather stood in the doorway and watched the child.

A loud whistle sounded. Down from the mountain ran goat after goat with Peter in the middle of them. With a shout of joy, Heidi rushed in among the flock.

When they all reached the hut, two lovely, slim goats, one white and one brown, came out from the others. They licked the grandfather's hands which held some salt.

"What are their names, Grandfather?" asked Heidi.

"The white one is called Schwänli or 'Little Swan,' and the brown one is called Bärli for 'Little Bear'." They put the goats in the shed and said good-night to Peter.

That night Heidi slept in her bed as soundly and

**Heidi Finds New Friends**

well as if it was the bed of a princess.

Heidi woke up early from hearing a loud whistle. She jumped out of bed and put on what she had worn the day before. Then she climbed down the ladder and ran outside. Peter was already there with his flock. The grandfather was bringing Little Swan and Little Bear out to join the other goats.

"Would you like to go to the pasture with Peter?" asked the grandfather. Heidi was pleased with the idea and jumped for joy. "First wash and be clean," the old man told her, "or else the sun will laugh at you when it is shining so brightly and sees you are dirty."

Heidi ran to a large tub of water standing before the door in the sunshine. She splashed and rubbed until she was shining.

"Come here, leader of the goats," the grandfather said to Peter. The Alm-Uncle put large pieces of bread and cheese in Peter's lunch sack for Heidi.

So the children and goats went merrily up the Alm. The wind in the night had blown away the last clouds. The sky was a deep blue everywhere.

The goats ran about, searching for tender green grass to eat. One goat, Little Snowflake, bleated so much that Heidi threw her arms around the small goat again and again. "Why does she cry so, Peter?" asked Heidi.

"Her mother was sold yesterday," answered Peter, carelessly.

"Oh, poor Little Snowflake," said Heidi, drawing the animal closely to her. "I will come with you every day and then you won't be alone. If you need any-

Heidi Befriends Schneehöpli

thing, you can come to me."

Little Snowflake stayed in Heidi's arms happily.

By far the prettiest and cleanest of the goats were Little Swan and Little Bear. They climbed prettily and gracefully. They found fine bushes to nibble.

The day passed happily away. Even the scream of the eagle was exciting. Heidi sat on the ground and silently looked at the bluebells and the rock roses as the sun went down behind the mountains. All the grass seemed colored with gold, and the cliffs above began to gleam and sparkle. Suddenly, Heidi jumped up and cried:

"Peter! It is on fire! All the mountains are burning — and the sky! Look at the reddish snow on the high, pointed rocks! The fire reaches up to the eagle's nest. Everything is on fire!"

Heidi was running back and forth in order to look on every side.

"It is always so," said Peter, "but there is no fire and now we must go." He whistled to the goats to follow.

As they went down the mountain, the rocks turned from gold to gray. Peter told Heidi that it would be the same tomorrow. That night at supper, she asked the grandfather about both the evening light and the eagle.

"You see, when the sun says good-night to the mountains," explained the grandfather, "he sends them his most beautiful rays. Then they may not forget him until he comes back in the morning."

"And the eagle," said the little girl, "why does he

The Fiery Sunset

scream all the time?"

"He is mocking the people down below because so many sit together in towns and make one another wicked. He's telling them to come to the mountaintop, as I did."

Day after day passed happily for Heidi. One night, a deep snow fell and the whole Alm was white. Peter struggled through the high snowdrifts to visit Heidi and the grandfather. "Without your army of goats, general, you'll have to bite the pencil in school," said the grandfather. Peter agreed.

As Peter was leaving, he said, "You must come and visit my grandmother. She wants to meet you, Heidi."

The next morning Heidi's first words were, "I must go down to the grandmother. She is waiting for me."

The grandfather wrapped Heidi in a warm cloak. Together they shot down the mountain in a sled to Peter's hut. "I will be back for you tonight," said the grandfather, as he started back up the Alm on foot.

Heidi stepped inside the one-room house. In the corner, an old bent grandmother sat at a spinning wheel. Heidi knew at once who the woman was and went straight to her. "How do you do, grandmother? I have come to visit you."

The grandmother took Heidi's hand and held it. "Are you Heidi? I am so happy you are here. When a person cannot see, it is so nice to hear a friendly word."

"You cannot see? Come outside in the bright

Heidi Visits the Blind Grandmother

snow," Heidi suggested.

"No, I am blind," said the grandmother. Heidi started to weep, but the grandmother began asking about the grandfather and so they had a happy visit. Near evening, Heidi saw that the shutter was swinging. "Oh, grandmother," she said, "my grandfather would fix that shutter for you. I will tell him about it."

Seeing that it was getting dark, Heidi remembered that her grandfather was coming to bring her home. She jumped up and said, "Good-night, grandmother. I must start home right away."

Heidi had only gone a few steps in the snow when the grandfather appeared. He wrapped her in a warm cloak and took her in his arms.

When Peter told the grandmother that the Alm-Uncle had met Heidi, the old woman said, "God be thanked that he is so good to her! I hope he will let her come again. How merrily she talks!"

"Grandfather," Heidi said as they climbed, "tomorrow we must take the hammer and the big nails. Fasten the shutter at the grandmother's house and drive a good many more nails there, for everything creaks and rattles."

"We must?" asked the grandfather. "Who told you that?"

"Nobody told me," said Heidi. "I just knew it. Everything is loose and it sounds as though the whole house is going to fall down. Surely you can help, grandfather. Only think how afraid the grandmother must be when the wind blows! She cannot sleep."

"Yes, Heidi," said the grandfather, "tomorrow we

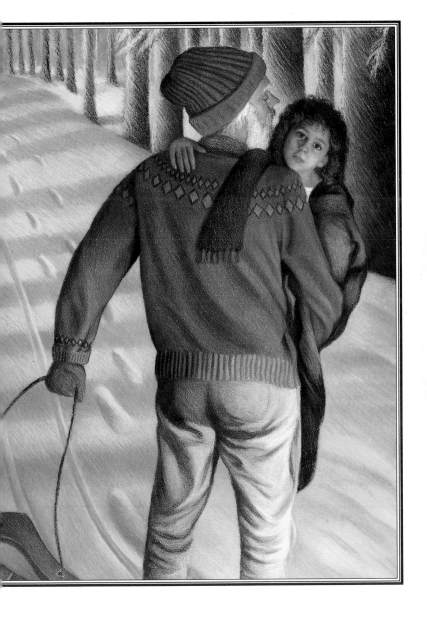

Homeward on a Snowy Night

will fix everything at the grandmother's house."

The next day, the grandfather kept his word; he hammered until he had driven the last nail he had in his pocket. As he worked, the grandmother exclaimed, "So the good Lord has not forgotten us! Is that really the Alm-Uncle hammering? Tell him that he must come in a moment and let me thank him."

Brigitte, Peter's mother, went to the door and thanked the grandfather, for he would not come in. From then on, there was no more creaking and rattling at the grandmother's house.

One day, a visitor came to the Alm — Aunt Dete. She was wearing a fine dress and a hat with a feather. Dete began by saying that she had heard of something wonderful for Heidi. Some rich relatives of her mistress had a fine house in Frankfurt and a sick daughter. They were looking for a small child to live with them and to be the lame girl's playmate. This would be a great chance for Heidi.

Grandfather looked at Dete coldly. "I'll have none of it."

At this, Dete went off like a rocket. "You will send her with me unless you want to go to court!"

"Silence!" roared the Uncle. "Take her and be gone! I hope never to see Heidi with feathers in her hat and words such as yours in her mouth!" The Uncle marched out of the house.

"You have made grandfather angry," snapped Heidi. "I won't go."

"Don't be stubborn like the goats," said her aunt, quickly packing Heidi's clothes. "It is lovely in

Grandfather's Rage

Frankfurt and you can come back here if you like. By then, your grandfather won't be so angry."

Because she had been promised she could return that night if she wished, Heidi followed her aunt down the Alm. As they passed the grandmother's hut, Peter yelled, "Where are you going, Heidi?" And grandmother called out of the window, "What's the matter? Don't take Heidi away!"

Heidi said, "I want to go to the grandmother."

Aunt Dete said, "We must hurry now, but you can bring the grandmother nice soft rolls from Frankfurt."

With this thought in mind, Heidi hurried on, planning to quickly return. After that day, the Alm-Uncle was always in a bad mood. The grandmother was heard sighing, "If only I could hear Heidi's voice once more before I die."

In Frankfurt, in the house of Herr Sesemann was the sick girl, Klara. She lay waiting restlessly in her wheelchair. "Isn't it time yet, Fraulein Rottenmeier?"

Before the stern housekeeper could reply, Dete and Heidi arrived. "What is your name?" asked the Fraulein.

"Heidi," said the girl.

"How old are you?" asked the housekeeper.

"I am eight now," replied Heidi.

"Only eight?" said the lady. "What books have you read?"

"I have never learned to read," said Heidi.

"Dete, how could you offer this child as a playmate?" said the lady. But Dete was already on her way out the door.

Klara's New Companion

Klara called to Heidi, "Did you want to come here?"

"No," said Heidi, "but tomorrow I am going back home with some white rolls for grandmother."

"You are a strange child!" said Klara. "They have brought you to Frankfurt to stay with me."

That evening at supper, Heidi pointed to the white roll on her dinner plate and asked, "Can I have that?" At the butler's nod, Heidi grabbed the roll and put it in her pocket.

"I see that you must be taught how to behave," said Fraulein Rottenmeir. There followed many rules. Finally, Klara saw that Heidi had fallen asleep and she began to laugh.

The next morning, after breakfast, Klara was rolled into the library. There was her teacher, Herr Kandidat. He was prepared to begin Heidi on the A-B-C's.

After a few moments, a frightful crash came from the library. Fraulein Rottenmeier rushed into the room. There on the floor lay books and copy-books, inkstand and tablecover — a stream of ink flowed across the length of the room.

Klara said, with a look of perfect delight, "Heidi did it, but not on purpose. Several carriages went by and she rushed out. Perhaps she hadn't seen carriages before."

The Fraulein ran out and found Heidi outside. She was confused; she thought she had heard wind in fir trees, but couldn't see any trees. Heidi was marched upstairs and was shown the mess. "You must not do

**An Innocent Accident**

that again," the Fraulein said angrily. "When you are having lessons, you must sit still and not move."

Heidi looked down at the spilled lessons sadly and promised not to do it again. But no matter how still Heidi sat, she never learned to read.

That afternoon while Klara was resting, Heidi went outside. She was hoping to see her beloved mountains. She walked around the city until a boy led her to a tall church. Holding the tower-keeper's hand, she climbed many steps to the top. The keeper lifted Heidi to a high window. She looked out — not to fir trees and mountains — but to a sea of roofs, towers and chimneys.

"It is not as I hoped," Heidi said, sadly.

As she walked down the stairs, Heidi saw a basket of kittens. The tower-keeper offered them to her. Heidi happily said yes. She asked that the kittens be sent to Klara's house.

The next day during lessons, a large basket for Klara was delivered. Suddenly, little kittens jumped out of the basket and ran around the room. They jumped over Herr Kandidat's boots, bit his trousers and climbed up Fraulein Rottenmeier's dress as she screamed for the servants. Meanwhile, Klara was thrilled. "What cute kittens!" she said.

Heidi ran after them into every corner.

Finally, the kittens were put back into the basket by the butler and taken to a hiding place away from Fraulein Rottenmeier. Herr Kandidat had to end his lessons for another day.

Finding that Heidi had had the kittens' brought to

Heidi's Gift for Klara

the house, the housekeeper angrily said that she would speak to Klara's father about all of the trouble.

While the days passed happily for Klara, Heidi longed for her home. She loved Klara, but she missed her grandfather, the grandmother and Peter.

However, there was one happy reason for staying: every day that Heidi stayed, she added another roll for the grandmother. Each night, she would quickly put in her pocket, the lovely white roll that lay beside her plate.

One day, Heidi's longing for home grew too great. In her room alone, she sat thinking that the Alm would be growing green and the flowers would be beginning to bloom. Hadn't her aunt said that she could go home whenever she wished?

She packed her dresses and her rolls and took her straw hat. As Heidi came down the stairs, Fraulein Rottenmeier stopped her in surprise.

"What is this?" she cried.

"I am only going home," said Heidi. "Grandmother is waiting to see me. Here the sun never says goodnight to the mountains and if the eagle ever should fly over Frankfurt, he'll scream his loudest at all the unhappy people!"

"What!" said Fraulein Rottenmeier. She called the butler. "Bring that bad little girl upstairs!" she said, pointing to Heidi. "And what is this? A pile of little rolls! These will be thrown out at once!"

Later, Heidi threw herself beside Klara's chair and began to cry very hard. Klara hugged her. She promised Heidi many more rolls for the grandmother

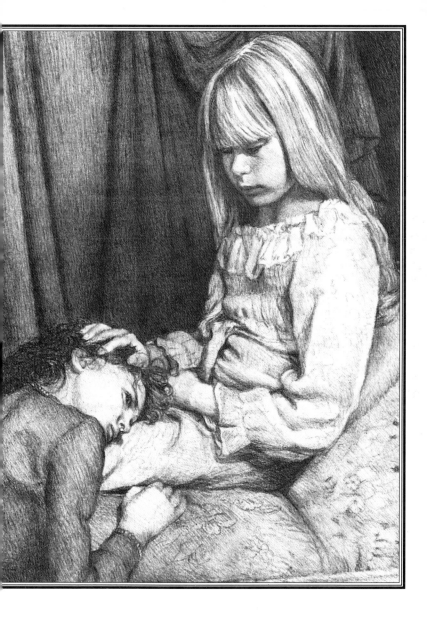

**Homesick**

whenever the time came that Heidi really would leave.

A few days later, Herr Sesemann arrived home. There was a great stir in the house and running up and down the stairs. The master of the house had returned.

He went first to Klara's room. Klara greeted her father with great tenderness for the two loved each other very much. Then Herr Sesemann reached out his hand to Heidi who had quietly gone into a corner. He said kindly, "And this is our little Swiss girl? Come here and give me your hand. Now tell me, are you and Klara good friends? You do not quarrel?"

"No, Klara is always good to me," answered Heidi.

"And Heidi never tries to quarrel, Papa." added Klara.

"That's good. I am glad to hear that. Now I must leave you, but I will see you again, as soon as I have my lunch, for I have not eaten today," said Klara's father.

In the dining room, Herr Sesemann was met by Fraulein Rottenmeier, a lady who looked a living picture of gloom. She told him about the trouble that Heidi had caused. Herr Sesemann, instead of getting angry, smiled and told Fraulein Rottenmeier that Heidi would remain.

"The girl seems normal and Klara enjoys her. If you are not able to deal with the child alone," Herr Sesemann added, "my mother is coming to visit very soon and she will be much help. As you know, everyone likes her, no matter how different they are."

**Herr Sesemann Returns Home**

Herr Sesemann had only two weeks at home, for his business called him to Paris. Klara and Heidi were sad when he left, but were happy about the coming visit of Klara's grandmamma.

Klara was delighted that her grandmamma was to visit. She talked so much that soon Heidi began to speak of "Grandmamma" coming. The servants collected footstools so that the lady might find one under her feet wherever she might wish to sit down.

When Klara's grandmamma, Frau Sesemann came, she took an instant liking to quiet Heidi. When Fraulein Rottenmeier complained that Heidi couldn't read, Grandmamma had the girl brought to her. Looking through Grandmamma's books, Heidi turned a new page and broke into tears. Grandmamma looked at the picture. It was a lovely green field where all sorts of animals were feeding and nibbling the green shrubs. In the middle stood a shepherd, leaning on a long staff. It seemed as if there was a golden light over it all, for the sun was just going down.

"Don't cry," said the old lady in a friendly way. "Dry your tears. Soon you will be able to read." The lady's eyes had such a look of kindness that they made Heidi feel quite at ease.

"People can't learn to read; it is too hard. Peter told me so," Heidi said.

"Heidi," said the grandmamma, patting the little girl's cheek, "I am going to tell you something. You have not learned to read yet, because you didn't think you could. But you can learn to read, and when you have learned, you shall have this book for your own.

**Grandmamma's Picture Book**

You can take it back to Peter and your friends on the Alm."

Heidi listened gladly. In a few weeks, Herr Kandidat told Frau Sesemann that Heidi had learned to read. The grandmamma gave her the book.

Heidi still longed to go home. Since the time Fraulein Rottenmeier had said how bad Heidi was — wanting to run away — a change had taken place in the child. She didn't want Herr Sesemann to think that she was bad. She thought that the grandmamma and Klara might think so, too. So Heidi dared tell no one how sad she was. Soon, she could no longer eat or sleep.

Heidi's sadness did not escape the grandmamma's notice. One day when Grandmamma was showing Heidi how to make doll dresses, the lady said very gently, "Heidi, what is the matter?"

"I cannot tell you," said Heidi sadly.

"Then, my child," said the grandmamma, "when you have a sorrow in your heart that you cannot tell to anyone, you must tell the dear God in heaven and ask for help."

"I have prayed the same prayer for many weeks and the dear Lord never helped me," the little girl said sadly.

"He will help you when He knows it is good for you to have what you ask. If the Lord no longer hears your voice in prayer, He may forget you. If you trust in Him, He will always help," explained Grandmamma.

A glad light came into Heidi's eyes. "Can I tell Him everything?"

**A Little Girl's Prayer**

At the grandmamma's nod, Heidi rushed to her room. She folded her hands and told the Lord everything that was in her heart, everything that made her sad. She asked Him to let her go home to her grandfather.

Too soon, the grandmamma's visit came to an end. In spite of Klara's friendship, Heidi burned with homesickness which she felt all winter long.

When spring came, something strange began to happen. Although every night the house was carefully locked, in the morning the front door was wide open. At first the servants blamed one another, but then shivers ran down their spines. They went by twos on jobs around the house. Fraulein Rottenmeier was sure that the house was haunted and sent for Klara's father.

Herr Sesemann was not a man who believed in ghosts, but he was worried that Klara might be frightened, so he came home.

That night, he sat up with his friend, Dr. Classen, Klara's doctor. They were armed with two guns and many candles. At midnight, they heard a noise and went to the front door.

There stood Heidi in her bare feet and white nightgown. She looked upset at the bright lights and was shivering from head to foot like a little leaf in the wind.

"Child, what does this mean?" asked Herr Sesemann.

White as snow from fright, Heidi stood there, hardly able to make a sound.

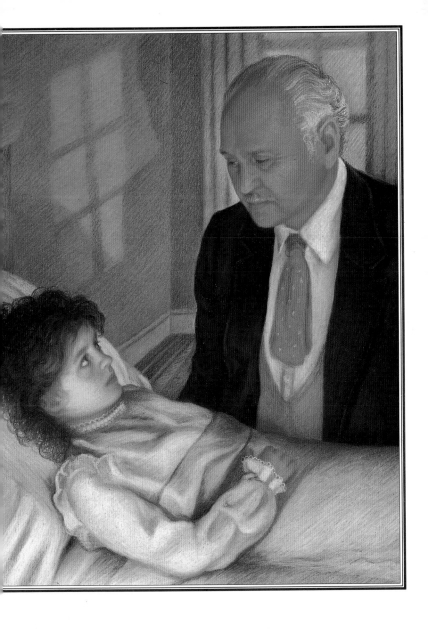

**The Doctor Tends to Heidi**

The doctor led the shaking child upstairs and put her to bed. Then he talked to Heidi. He found that while she had no pains, she did have something that bothered her. He decided she was homesick for her grandfather and the Alm.

Later he told Klara's father, "Heidi has been sleep-walking. She must be sent home or she will become very ill."

Herr Sesemann rose from his chair. "I will send her home right away, doctor." He quickly gave orders that Heidi be sent home at once. Klara was very sad when she was told, but her father promised that they would all visit Heidi soon.

Heidi was so excited when she learned that she was going home. She ran to Klara, who was watching the packing of Heidi's trunk. And she showed her many things which were being sent with her: dresses and aprons, underwear and sewing materials. Joyfully, Klara held up a basket of white rolls for the blind grandmother, and Heidi jumped for joy.

After riding all day on a train, Heidi at last arrived on the Alm. She ran up the mountain as fast as she could.

She ran first to Peter's hut. She entered saying, "Here I am, grandmother. Look what I have brought!"

With that, Heidi put a dozen soft, white rolls into the grandmother's lap.

"Oh child, what a blessing," said the old lady. Heidi promised to return the next day, but now she wanted to go to her grandfather. As she climbed, she saw the fir trees and her grandfather. He was smoking

**A Joyous Reunion**

his pipe beside the house. Before the Alm-Uncle could see what was coming, Heidi rushed up to him, threw her basket on the ground and hugged the old man. She was unable to say anything, except, "Grandfather! Grandfather!"

For the first time in years, the grandfather's eyes were wet. They held each other tenderly. Then Heidi showed Herr Sesemann's letter to her grandfather.

That night, Heidi slept soundly for the first time in months for she was at home again on the Alm.

Heidi went the next day, as promised, to the blind grandmother. The little girl said "Grandmother, I can read well now. Shall I read out of your book?"

"Oh, yes!" said the grandmother, filled with joy. "Can you really do that?"

Heidi climbed upon a chair and took down the book. It was covered with dust, for it had been laid there for a long time. She wiped it clean, then read from the grandmother's book of church.

"Oh Heidi," said the grandmother, "that gives me light in my heart again! How much good you have done me!"

That night at home, Heidi said, "Grandfather, how good God was not to let me leave Frankfurt sooner! If He had, I never would have learned to read! Now I shall always pray as the grandmamma told me. If He does not do as I ask, then He is surely planning something better. We will pray every day, Grandfather, won't we?"

"If someone has left God," said the grandfather, "can he ever go back or has God forgotten him?"

**Grandfather Prays for God's Forgiveness**

"God will always forgive us." said Heidi.

Later, when Heidi was sound asleep, her grandfather stood beside her bed. He folded his hands and bowed his head. "Father," he prayed, "I have sinned against Heaven. I am no longer worthy to be called thy son." Great tears rolled down his cheeks.

Sunday morning, the Alm-Uncle stood in church in Dorfli, hand in hand with Heidi. After church, they visited the parson. In the street, a very friendly feeling for the Alm-Uncle arose, as if the people of Dorfli were welcoming a friend home.

While Heidi's life was filled with happiness, hard days had come to Klara. Her health was very bad and now it was September and already cool on the Alps. Herr Sesemann and Dr. Classen decided that Klara could not make her long-awaited trip to visit Heidi. To cheer up Klara, Herr Sesemann thought of a happy plan.

"Doctor," he said, "you shall make the trip and visit Heidi in our place."

The doctor was very surprised at this plan and would have said no, but Herr Sesemann gave him no time. He grabbed his friend by the arm and led him into Klara's room.

Klara was very happy to see the doctor, but tears began to swim in her eyes when she was told that she couldn't visit Heidi. However, she took comfort from her father's plan. "Doctor, you must tell me every-thing about the Alm when you return: what Heidi is doing, about her grandfather and Peter and the

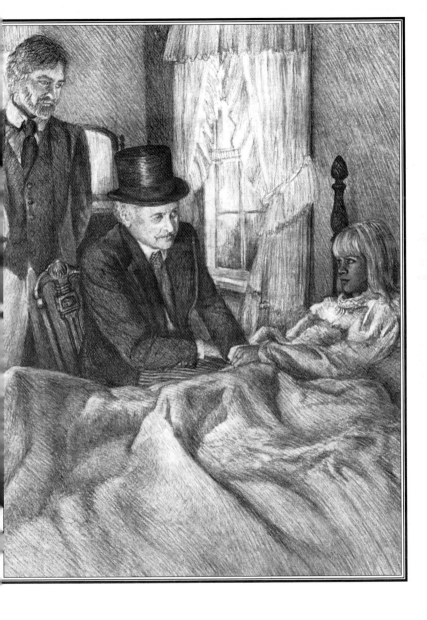

Klara Faces Disappointment

goats," she begged.

As the doctor left, he met Fraulein Rottenmeier returning from her walk. They both tried to make room for the other at the door, until the lady's large shawl was caught by a gust of wind that blew her at full sail against the doctor, then beyond, then back. The doctor said he was sorry so nicely, the Fraulein was in a good mood when she reached Klara's room.

That very day, Klara and the Fraulein began to pack gifts for Dr. Classen to bring to Heidi. There was a thick warm coat with a hood for Heidi, a warm shawl and a big box of cakes for the grandmother, a bag of tobacco for the grandfather and a huge sausage for Peter. Last came a number of surprises for Heidi: little bags, packages and boxes which Klara had lots of fun collecting.

Since she was expecting Klara and her family from Frankfurt, Heidi cleaned until everything shone and sparkled. Today, though, it seemed she would never finish. It was a lovely morning and the sparkling sunlight invited her outside. Finally, she finished her chores and went outside.

Suddenly, she called, "Grandfather, they are coming! And the doctor first of all." She raced down the mountain to greet her friend. Dr. Classen held out his hands and she greeted him warmly.

"But where is Klara and her family?" Heidi asked.

"I have had to come alone," said the doctor, "for Klara is too ill to make the journey. But they shall come next spring."

Heidi saw that the doctor looked sad. Although

**A Surprising Welcome**

she was also disappointed, she said, "Well, it won't be long until spring. And Klara will like that trip better."

Then Heidi and the doctor walked up to the hut. The grandfather gave the doctor a big welcome and they had a simple meal of a jug of milk, shining golden toasted cheese and thin slices of rosy meat which had been dried in the pure air.

Soon someone came up the mountain carrying a big package on his back. "Here are the gifts from Frankfurt," said the doctor. Heidi danced around the box and ran from one thing to another.

The two men talked like old friends. When it was time for the doctor to return to Dorfli for the night, the grandfather invited him to spend the beautiful Fall days on the Alm and the doctor accepted.

Early the next morning, the doctor climbed the mountain from Dorfli with Peter and his goats. In a friendly way, he tried to talk with the goat boy, but Peter was silent. So they walked quietly up to the Alm hut, where Heidi stood waiting.

"Are you coming with me, Heidi?" asked Peter.

"Of course, if the doctor will come," said Heidi. Peter looked angrily at the doctor.

The grandfather gave them a heavy dinner bag with a large piece of meat for Heidi and the doctor. As they climbed the mountain, Peter gave angry looks to the doctor, but the doctor did not see them.

When they reached the sunny pasture, the doctor sat beside Heidi on the ground. Within the sound of the goat bells, they enjoyed the morning breeze blowing through the last of the bluebells and the giant

**A Lasting Friendship**

eagle flying in wide circles above.

"Suppose a person brought a sad heart from Frankfurt to the Alm," began the doctor. He was thinking of the death of his daughter a month before.

"He must tell the dear Lord," said Heidi, "and wait for his answer."

"That is a beautiful faith," the doctor said.

During this time, Peter became worried the longer Heidi stayed with Dr. Classen. However, at lunchtime, they left most of the food for Peter. Then he was very ashamed of himself for being rude and angry at the doctor. In the end, he decided to make friends with Dr. Classen.

The doctor left in the Fall as the weather began to get cold. He told the grandfather and Heidi that he wanted the clear air and sun of the Alps for Klara.

When the snow came, it was heavy. The windows of the huts were level with the snow and the doors completely disappeared. Peter had to crawl out a window and sweep the snow away to free the front door.

However, the Alm-Uncle would not be on the Alm this winter. He had decided to go down to Dorfli with Heidi and the goats.

Heidi and the grandfather moved into a large house. In one corner stood a big stove, reaching to the ceiling.

Heidi went to school and made friends with the children. Peter was also supposed to be in school, but the snow made it to hard for him to get there. Somehow it was never too cold to visit Heidi. She scolded him for his laziness.

Through A Little Girl's Eyes

As winter passed, Heidi made many trips to visit the blind grandmother and to read to her. The grandmother spent most of her time in bed now, as the rest of the hut was too cold for her. Heidi knelt on the bed and read one beautiful verse after another. She knew them very well and enjoyed reading them herself when she couldn't visit the grandmother.

Later, Heidi thought of the hard life of the grandmother. If the grandmother could have the verses read to her every day, she would be happy. But Peter couldn't read — yet.

The next day, when Peter came to visit Heidi, she ran to meet him. "Peter," she said, "you must learn to read, so you can read to your grandmother."

"I can't learn," said Peter. "It is too hard."

"I don't believe that," said Heidi. "The grandmamma in Frankfurt knew that it wasn't true."

"Don't want to," grumbled Peter.

Heidi pulled out her book and read in a strong voice, " 'If A, B, C, you do not know, before the school board you will go'."

"I will not," said Peter angrily.

But soon, Peter began to learn.

Thus the winter days passed. Peter went to school often and studied. After he worked hard on his lesson, he was always invited to stay for supper with Heidi.

One day in the springtime, Peter ran home from school and cried, "I can do it! I can read!"

He took the hymnbook and read with delight.

The day after, Peter's class had a reading lesson.

**The Schoolmaster's Surprise**

"Peter," said the teacher, "shall we pass you by, as usual, or would you like to try and stammer out a few lines?"

Instead, Peter began to read line after line without stopping. The teacher looked at him in wonder. Peter had learned to read!

May had come. Heidi and grandfather moved back to the Alm. Warm, bright sunshine lay on the mountain, and the joyous spring wind blew through the fir trees. From the workshop behind the house came the sound of busy hammering and sawing. The grandfather was making chairs for Heidi's guests, who were to come from Frankfurt.

Soon, a letter arrived for Heidi from Klara, saying that all would be arriving soon. Heidi was filled with joy as she got ready for her guests. This made Peter very unhappy, for when Heidi had company, she would spend less time with him.

June came with its warmer sun and long, light days. Heidi was outside when she saw something that made her cry, "Grandfather! Grandfather! Come here and see! They are coming!"

A strange parade was making its way up the Alm. First came two men carrying a chair in which sat a young girl wrapped up in ever so many shawls. Then came a grand lady, the grandmamma, on a fine white horse. She was looking around in every direction and talking eagerly with the young person walking by her side. Next came a man pushing an empty wheelchair. Last of all walked a porter who had clothes, shawls and furs piled higher than his head in a basket on his

**Klara Approaches the Alm**

back.

Heidi ran to her friends and hugged them with great happiness. Klara looked around her, thrilled with the beauty of the Alm. Grandmamma cried happily, "How well Heidi looks — like a June rose! A king might happily live on the Alm," she said to the grandfather. The grandfather picked up Klara and gently put her in the wheelchair. Heidi pushed Klara to the bluebells, then to the fir trees. "Oh, how beautiful!" cried Klara, again and again.

Heidi picked great bunches of flowers for Klara. "If you could come to the pasture with us, there are many more," Heidi said, her eyes shining with joy.

The happy day went on. Klara surprised her grandmamma by enjoying a meal, while they talked like old friends. "It is our mountain air," said the grandfather, well pleased.

Finally, the grandmamma looked towards the west and said, "Klara, we must be going back to Dorfli. The sun is going down."

"Oh, grandmamma," cried Klara, "if only I could stay."

The Alm-Uncle then looked over at the grandmamma. "If you do not mind," he said, "Klara could certainly stay with us for some time."

"What a lovely idea," said the grandmamma. "How Klara would enjoy it!" Heidi and Klara screamed joyfully. The grandmamma went down the mountain to stay in the town. Peter came by with the goats, also headed down the Alm. Klara greeted each goat as Peter stood throwing mean looks her way.

A View of Hope

That night, the grandfather carried Klara up to the hayloft, where her bed was made up next to Heidi's. As Klara waited for sleep, she stared out through the window at the stars. They twinkled and winked at her from the heavens, and she said quietly,

"Oh, Heidi, see, it is just as if we were riding in the sky in a high carriage!"

The next morning, the grandfather carried Klara outside and settled her into her wheelchair. Shortly after, he brought two bowls full of foaming, snow-white milk. He handed one to Klara and one to Heidi and watched as they both drank eagerly. Klara had never tasted goat's milk before. She found it as sweet and spicy as if sugar and cinnamon were added to it.

Then Heidi and Klara sat under the fir trees and wrote a letter to grandmamma. At noon, the grandfather appeared with bowls of milk for lunch. He said that they must remain outside as long as there was a ray of sunlight for Klara. The girls spent the day talking about all the events since Heidi had left Frankfurt.

Finally, Peter came down the mountain with his goats.

"Good-night, Peter!" Heidi said, when she saw that he wouldn't stop to talk.

"Good-night, Peter!" called out Klara, kindly.

Peter angrily drove on his goats.

Three weeks passed, each day Klara grew stronger. She said, "As long as I can remember, I ate only because I had to, and everything tasted like cod-liver oil. Here I can hardly wait to eat."

Under the Singing Fir Trees

Grandfather asked Klara to try to stand a little. She did as he wished, although it hurt very much.

One day, the grandfather promised Klara that he would take her wheelchair to the pasture in the morning. When Peter heard the news, he was very angry. He did not want Klara to go with Heidi and him.

Early the next day, he went to Heidi's and saw the wheelchair was outside. Like a madman, he rushed at the chair and pushed it down the mountain. It turned over and over and broke into many pieces.

Peter rushed up the Alm, as if he had wings and did not once stop until he found a great blackberry bush behind which he could hide. He did not want the uncle to catch sight of him.

When Heidi found that the chair was gone, she thought the wind had blown it down the mountain. The grandfather carried Klara up to the pasture and then went down to see about the chair. Peter was frightened to see them because he was sure that his secret had been found out.

The girls watched the eagle rock himself on the wind up into blue sky. Now and then, a little goat would come and lie down near them for a while. They were very happy.

Heidi looked around and found a meadow of flowers. "Oh, Klara," Heidi called, "you must see this. It is so beautiful. If only you could walk." Then an idea came to the little girl. "Peter!" she called, "come here! Perhaps we can carry Klara."

Heidi placed one of Klara's arms about her neck, and Peter took the other, but they were too unlike in

The First Step

size. Klara tried to step on her feet a little, but she could not move them forward. "Just stamp right down," said Heidi, "then it will hurt you less."

Klara obeyed and took one step and then another. "Oh!" she said, "that didn't hurt nearly so much! Oh, see! I can! I can take steps! I can walk!"

When the grandfather came up to carry Klara down to the hut, Heidi greeted him with the wonderful news. With the grandfather's help, Klara showed him. Then he carried her down to the hut, for he knew that after such a day, she needed rest.

The days which followed were by far the most beautiful which Klara had passed on the Alm. Every morning, she awoke thinking, "I am well! I am well! I do not need to sit in a wheelchair any longer. I can go about by myself."

Every day she took longer and longer walks. The grandfather made her thick slices of bread and butter.

However, Peter felt so guilty that he was frightened all of the time. Any moment, he felt, a policeman from Frankfurt might rush out from behind any bush and take him to jail.

At the end of the week, grandmamma returned to the mountain. Seeing her come, Heidi slipped from the bench outside. Klara leaned on her shoulder, and the two calmly walked forward. Joyfully Grandmamma thanked the grandfather for helping Klara.

Moments later, another surprise followed as Herr Sesemann paid a surprise visit. Klara's father stopped short when he saw a healthy Klara — walking. Suddenly, big tears fell from his eyes.

A Father's Dream Come True

"Papa, don't you know me anymore? Am I so changed?" asked Klara. Herr Sesemann rushed forward and threw his arms around Klara, then Heidi, and then Klara again.

While Herr Sesemann thanked the Alm-Uncle and shook his hand, the grandmamma saw Peter, hiding behind a tree. "Come, my lad," she called kindly. "Don't be afraid."

Peter, shaking and thinking that he was caught, came forward and told the grandmother that he broke the wheelchair. The grandmamma, after hearing his story, understood. She forgave him for being so angry and so foolish. To reward Peter for being honest, she gave him two coins.

The following morning, Klara shed hot tears, because she had to go away from the beautiful Alm. There she had felt better than she had ever felt in her life. Heidi hugged her and said, "It will be summer again soon, and you will come back. It will be more beautiful than ever, for you will be able to walk all the time and we can go to the pasture every day."

Herr Sesemann called to the children, for it was time to go. This time the grandmamma's white horse came for Klara, because she no longer needed a wheelchair.

Heidi stood at the edge of the slope and waved her hand to Klara until the last speck of horse and rider had gone.

After Klara's visit, the doctor moved to the town of Dorfli where Heidi and her grandfather stayed in the winter. Klara grew well and strong and came back every summer. The grandmother lived a good many years and enjoyed hearing Peter and Heidi read to her. Heidi and grandfather lived happily ever after.

The Parting of Two Friends

# ABOUT THE ILLUSTRATOR

Donna Pacinelli is a distinguished young artist who divides her busy schedule between illustrating and teaching in a school for artists. Interested in art at an early age, she spent her early years experimenting with various media. Her sensitive work in pastels and pencil drawing has appeared on book covers and in many galleries in the United States. Now located in Pennsylvania, Donna and her husband, also an artist, have done extensive work restoring Victorian houses to their original splendor, as well as exhibiting their work in gallery shows together. *Heidi* is Donna's first book for Unicorn Publishing.